Michael Berenstain's
HOP, WADDLE, SWIM!

A GOLDEN BOOK • NEW YORK

Western Publishing Company, Inc., Racine, Wisconsin 53404

Hop,

waddle,

swim,

crawl.

2

Climb,

leap,

swing,

fall.

Charging
rhino,

ostrich
strolling.

4

Jogging camel,

hedgehog rolling.

Bucking
bronco

and pony
prancing,

6

while circus poodles
are disco dancing.

A hoot owl soaring
through the sky,

past Santa's reindeer
dashing by!

9

Beavers paddle

and otters
slide,

while
storks go
wading

and swans just glide.

11

Pelicans flap
above the waves—

bats flitter out of caves.

13

Hamsters scamper in their wheels.

Gorillas slip
on banana peels.

Tigers pace,

while wolves lope.

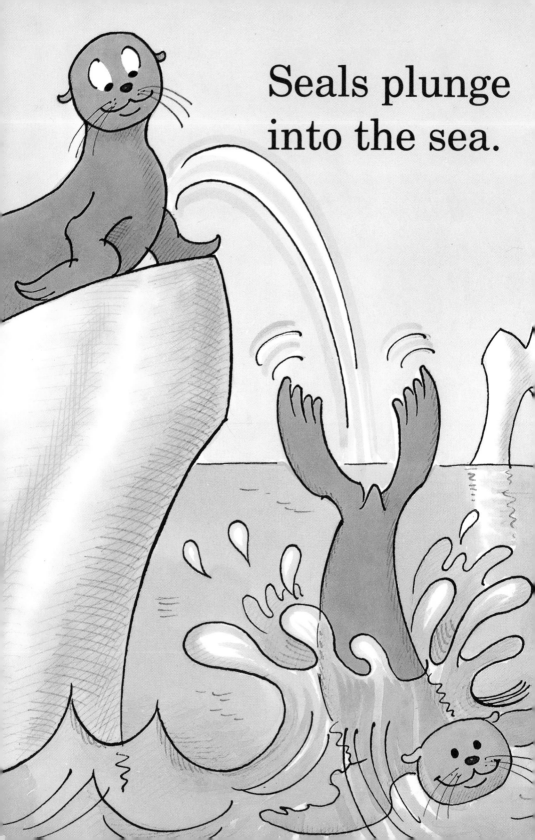

Seals plunge
into the sea.

Bees buzz

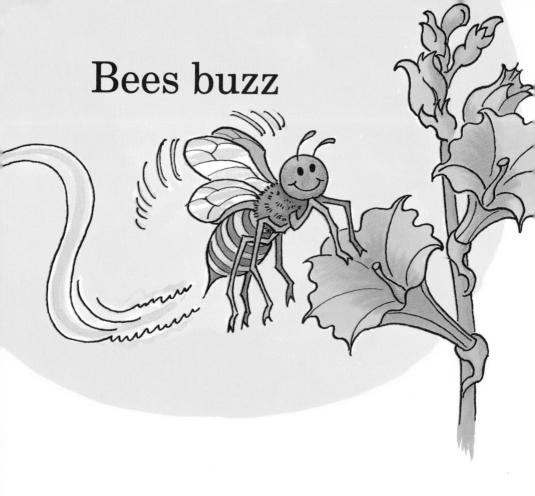

and worms wiggle.

Snakes slither,

but tadpoles wriggle.

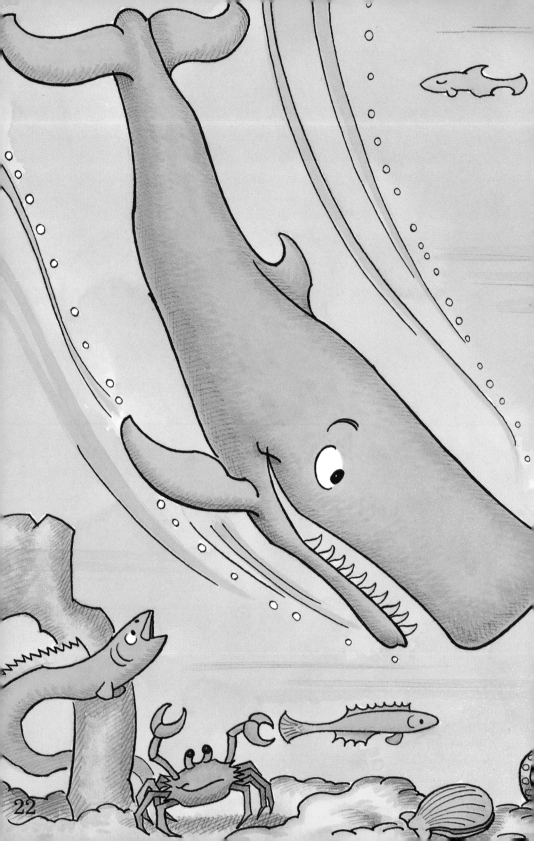

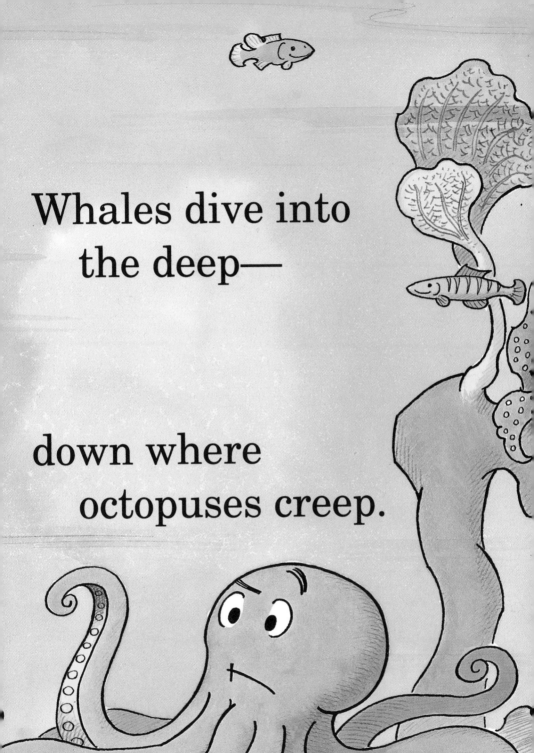

Whales dive into
the deep—

down where
octopuses creep.

Birds fly

and mice scurry.

Jaguars
spring

and panthers
pounce.

Kangaroos
jump

and bunnies bounce.

Waterbugs skitter, skip, and skate.

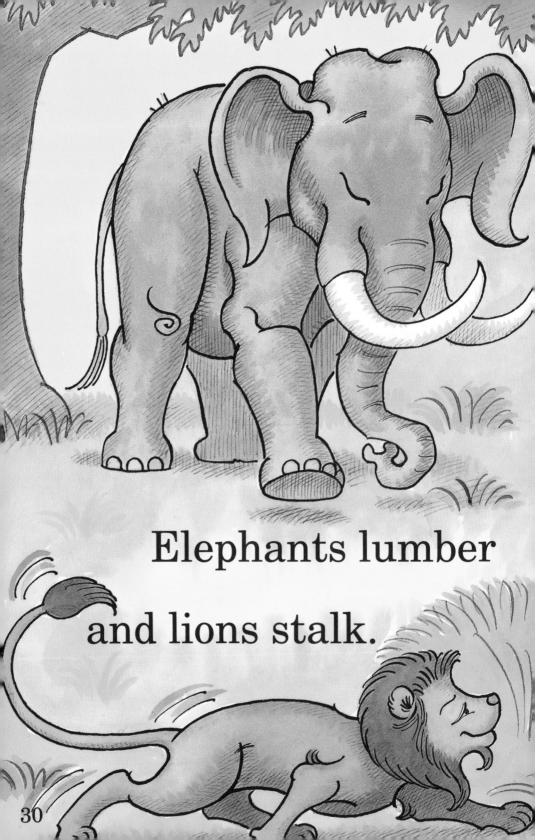

Elephants lumber

and lions stalk.

Zebras gallop,

but *I* . . .

31